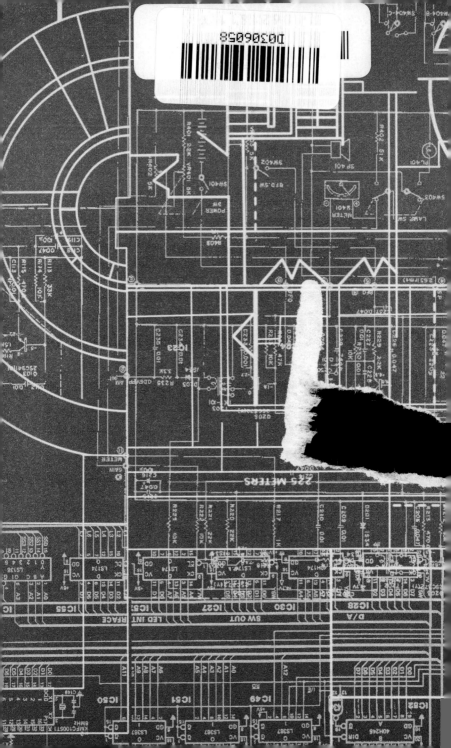

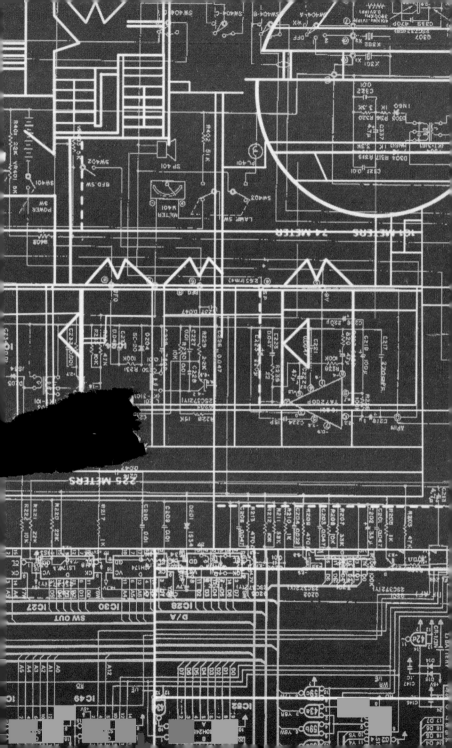

GENERATOR REX

MIRROR
MIRROR

EGMONT

EGMONT

We bring stories to life

First published in Great Britain 2011
by Egmont UK Limited
239 Kensington High Street
London W8 6SA

Cartoon Network, the logo, GENERATOR REX and all
related characters and elements are trademarks of and
© 2011 Cartoon Network.

Written by Barry Hutchison

ISBN 978 1 4052 6100 5

47615/1

Printed and bound in Great Britain

The Forest Stewardship Council (FSC) is an international,
non-governmental organisation dedicated to promoting
responsible management of the world's forests. FSC operates
a system of forest certification and product labelling that
allows consumers to identify wood and wood-based products
from well managed forests.

For more information about Egmont's paper buying policy,
please visit www.egmont.co.uk/ethicalpublishing.
For more information about the FSC,
please visit their website at www.fsc.org

MIX
Paper
FSC FSC® C018306

MIRROR
WIRROR

CHAPTER 1

'**C**OME ON, REX, it'll be awesome!'

Rex shrugged and jabbed his thumbs against the video game controller in his hands. On screen, a zombie's head exploded. '*This* is already awesome,' he said. 'It couldn't be any ... awesomer.'

'That's not even a word,' Noah said. 'And, seriously, sitting around playing video games all night? That's your idea of fun?'

'Yes,' Rex nodded. He stuffed some popcorn into his mouth. 'Yes, it is.'

Noah leaned forward in his chair and tried to make his friend see sense. 'I'm going to spell it out to you, Rex. It's a *fun ... fair.*'

'That's not spelling it out, that's just saying it slowly,' Rex mumbled, through a mouthful of popcorn kernels.

'That's not the point! The point is, it's got fun right there in the title. *Fun* fair. Does "video game" have the word "fun" in the title?' Noah asked.

'Not the last time I checked,' Rex replied. He shot a zombie through the knees and watched it fall, face-first, onto the ground.

'Nice shot,' Noah admitted, grudgingly.

'Thanks. I'm all about the knee-shots.'

An idea struck Noah. 'There'll be zombie-shooting at the fair,' he said.

Rex raised an eyebrow. 'Really?'

Noah sighed. 'No, not really. I made that up. But there'll be other stuff. *Better* than zombie-killing.'

'Nothing's better than zombie-killing,' Rex told him.

'Oh yeah? What about roller-coasters? And chair-o-planes? And bungee drops? They've got something called the Wheel of Terror.' Noah said it again for emphasis. '*The Wheel of Terror*, Rex! I don't even know what that is, but I don't think I can live another day without finding out.'

The action on screen froze as Rex hit the pause button on the control pad. 'You know I can turn whole parts of my body into machines, right?'

Noah nodded. 'Of course I know!'

'I've got the Boogie Pack that lets me fly, the Rex

Ride that lets me go faster than a racing car ...'

'Yeah, so?'

'Then there's the others, too. Punk Busters, Smackhands, a giant sword, a crazy-cool cannon that can shoot pretty much anything ...'

'I know all this!' Noah said. 'What's your point?'

'My point is, how is a roller-coaster supposed to compete with all that? Why would I bother going up and down and around on a metal track when I can do all that in mid-air, like, a thousand times faster, and without having to pay for it?'

Noah looked annoyed. 'Uh, well, maybe because some of us *can't* do any of that stuff? You might get to zip around the place going all high-tech all the time, but what about me?'

Rex saw the hurt on his friend's face. 'Hey, Noah, I'm sorry,' he said. 'I guess I didn't think of it like that.'

'Yeah, well, don't worry about it,' Noah said. He leaned back in his chair and folded his arms. 'Just forget it.'

Rex looked at the motionless zombies on screen, then back to his friend. 'You know, maybe the fair would be better than being stuck in here?'

Noah's face brightened. 'So, what, you'll come?'

'We can try,' Rex said. 'Me and Bobo have been sneaking out a lot lately, so Six has got the place locked down pretty tight. It won't be easy to get out. *Bobo!*'

There was a grunt from Rex's bed. Bobo, the talking Evo chimp, opened one eye. 'What is it, kid? I'm trying to catch up on my beauty sleep here.'

'Get your hat,' Rex told him. 'We're stepping out for some fresh air.'

Even as the hand clamped down on Rex's shoulder, he knew it belonged to Agent Six.

'And where do you think you're going?' Six asked.

Rex stood up from the air duct he had been about to crawl inside. There were few windows in Providence base, and the doors were heavily guarded. Even the ventilation system was alarmed and magnetically sealed. This should have stopped anyone breaking in or out, but Rex wasn't just anyone. His nanites had taken care of the security systems in a matter of seconds. Noah and Bobo had already clambered into the air duct. Rex could hear them thudding their way along the narrow passageway.

'Hey, Six,' Rex said, raising his voice to try to drown out the din his friends were making. He thought fast. 'We, uh, I mean *I* was just... checking the air conditioning.'

'And why were you doing that?' asked Six.

'Because,' began Rex, 'I'm thinking of becoming a... heating engineer.' He replayed the excuse in his head. 'Yeah, that works,' he said.

Six sighed. 'Bobo. Noah. Get back here.'

The thudding stopped. There was silence for a moment, and then Noah's voice echoed out from within the duct. 'Um, I don't think I can turn round.'

'Hey, get your butt out of my face, kid!' Bobo said.

'They're checking the system for blockages,' Rex explained, weakly.

'You can cut the excuses,' Six said. 'You were trying to sneak out. Again.'

Rex hung his head. 'Yeah,' he confessed. 'There's a fair in town and Noah thought it'd be cool if we went. But I know, too dangerous, I shouldn't go wandering off, *yadda, yadda, yadda.*'

He turned and spoke into the air duct. 'Come on,

guys,' he said. 'Six isn't going to let us go.'

'You can go.'

'You don't have to apologise, Six, I know it's ... Wait. Did you say I could go?'

Six nodded. 'I know being stuck in here isn't much fun, Rex, and at least this way I'll know where you are.'

Rex grinned. 'I always did like you, Six,' he said.

'But you keep your wits about you at all times,' Six instructed. 'And you're back here for curfew.'

'What time's curfew?' Rex asked.

'When I call you and tell you it is,' Agent Six said.

With a shrug, Rex clambered through the window. 'We'd better get moving, then. Thanks, Six.' Rex knelt down by the open vent.

'You know you're free to use the door now, right?' Six asked.

'Yeah, but where's the fun in that?'

Six gave him a curt nod. 'Fair enough,' he said. 'Oh, but Rex?'

'Yeah?'

'Try not to get into trouble.'

'Hey,' Rex replied, with a wink. 'I'll see what I can do!'

CHAPTER 2

'**S**O, THAT'S THE WHEEL OF TERROR, HUH?'
Noah stared, open-mouthed, at the fairground ride in front of them. It was a normal, everyday merry-go-round. Instead of colourful, jolly-looking horses to ride on, though, this one had dark-coloured, mean-looking horses. And, Noah hated to admit, they didn't even look all *that* mean.

'Terrifying,' Bobo snorted. His nose twitched. 'Hey, I smell hot dogs. Does anyone else smell hot dogs?' He locked onto the scent. On cue, his stomach began to rumble. 'I'll be right back.'

'The flyer said it was one of the scariest rides in the whole country,' Noah groaned, as Bobo headed for the hot dog stand.

'For three-year-olds, maybe,' Rex said. 'Really nervous ones.'

He turned and took in the rest of the fairground. They had billed the Wheel of Terror as one of the highlights, so Rex wasn't holding out much hope for the rest of the place.

He could tell, at first glance, that his expectations were right. The fairground was old and dirty, with paint peeling from most of the rides. A few dozen people wandered around. They all looked disappointed, but none of them quite as disappointed as Noah.

'Hey, come on, it's not that bad,' Rex said. He gave Noah a friendly nudge. 'They've still got the roller-coaster, right?'

Both boys looked up at the large metal track that banked and curved around the whole fairground. The smile slowly returned to Noah's face.

'Yeah,' he said. 'They've still got the roller-coaster.'

'Closed? What do you mean, it's closed?'

'I mean it ain't open,' growled the man running the roller-coaster. 'The track's broken and the motor's fried. It ain't goin' nowhere.'

Noah's shoulders slumped. First the Wheel of Terror turned out to be a kiddie ride, and now the roller-coaster was out of action. Maybe Rex had been right. Maybe they *should* have stayed in and played video games.

'Let's just go home,' Noah said. 'I'm sorry I dragged you all the way out here.'

Rex was determined to make his friend feel better. 'Come on, it's not all bad,' he said.

'Man, this place sucks,' Bobo grunted, as he shuffled up to join them. 'Can you believe they only had five hot dogs left? How's a monkey supposed to get through the night on five hot dogs?'

Rex glared at him. 'What?' Bobo asked. 'You guys didn't want any, did you?'

'No,' Rex said, through gritted teeth. 'I was just saying to Noah how great this place is.'

Bobo blinked. 'You were?' He finally grasped what Rex was doing. 'Oh, I mean, you *were*, right. This place is great.'

'Thanks for trying, guys,' Noah said. 'But it's a washout.'

'No it isn't,' Rex insisted. He put an arm round Noah's shoulder. 'It's still got the bungee drop.'

There was a loud *twang* of elastic, followed by a short scream.

'You know what?' Rex said, fixing his smile

in place. 'I think we'll give the bungee drop a miss. But that still leaves the chair-o-planes and ... and ...' His eyes frantically scanned the fairground. 'Look! A test-your-strength machine!'

Rex hurried over to the machine. It stood almost four metres tall, with a round red bell at the top. There was a pressure pad at the base of the contraption, and a large sledgehammer leaning against the side.

'Step right up, put your strength to the test and win a prize of shimmering gold!' cried a man in a bowler hat standing beside the machine.

'Gold?' Noah spluttered. 'Seriously?'

'You heard me correctly, friend, hit the pad and ring that bell and you'll take home a golden prize.'

Noah handed over his money, then rolled up his sleeves. He lifted the hammer, staggering a little under its weight. 'OK,' he said. 'Here goes!'

THUD!

Noah brought the hammer down hard on the pad. The man in the bowler hat stood with his hand behind the machine, watching the strength gauge race upwards.

Up and up it went, and Noah's eyes became wider

and wider. He was going to do it. He was going to ring –

The man's arm gave a twitch and the gauge stopped just a few centimetres from the bell, then fell back down to the bottom. 'Ah, bad luck, friend, you were so close!'

'Hey, you cheated,' protested Rex, who had seen the man's arm move at exactly the same time the gauge had stopped rising. 'You've got a switch back there that stops it.'

'Of all the nerve!' the man spluttered. 'How dare you accuse me of cheating?'

'We want the gold,' Rex insisted. 'He won it, fair and square.'

'You want the prize?' the man retorted. 'Then you gotta ring the bell!'

Rex stuffed a hand in his pocket and pulled out some coins. He tossed them to the man in the hat. 'OK,' he said. 'I'll ring the bell.'

The man watched Rex take up position in front of the machine. 'You'll need the hammer,' he snorted.

'No thanks,' said Rex. The nanites in his body surged, and two enormous metal fists formed around his hands. 'I brought my own.'

With a grunt, Rex brought one of the Smackhands down on the pressure pad. The gauge shot up like a rocket. There was a loud *clang* as the bell was torn free. They all watched it sail higher and higher into the air, until it was out of sight.

'Now,' said Rex, retracting the Smackhands back into his body, 'about my friend's gold?'

The man in the bowler hat said nothing as he reached behind the machine and pulled out a small plastic bag full of water. Inside, swimming around, was a tiny goldfish.

'Gold,' the man said. He flashed them a nasty grin. 'Enjoy.'

Rex was about to pull out the Smackhands again, but the excited look on Noah's face stopped him.

'A goldfish,' Noah laughed. 'We won a goldfish. Maybe this place isn't so bad, after all.'

Rex and Bobo exchanged a look. 'Don't take much to please that guy,' Bobo muttered.

'Hey, look, there's a Hall of Mirrors,' said Noah, suddenly full of enthusiasm again. 'Let's check it out.'

Rex laughed. It was good to see Noah happy

again. 'Lead the way,' he said, and they made their way towards the Hall of Mirrors, completely unaware of the dangers that lurked within.

CHAPTER 3

EX LOOKED AT HIS LEGS. They were barely ten centimetres long. His forehead, however, more than made up for them. It stretched around a metre in height, from the top of his eyebrows to where his hair started.

'Lookin' good, kid,' Bobo said.

Rex looked at Bobo's reflection in the mirror beside him and burst out laughing. The chimp's arms were ridiculously short, and his head was the size of an orange.

'Right back at ya,' Rex grinned. '*The Pinhead* is a good look for you.'

They had been in the Hall of Mirrors for ten minutes now, checking out their warped reflections in every mirror in the place. They had gone from looking like waddling penguins to towering like stick-thin giants. They'd had long legs, stubby arms, enormous feet and heads that came to a sharp point. And that was just the first mirror.

'Check it out,' Noah said. 'I'm a human giraffe!'

Rex leaned to the left and looked at Noah's reflection. His friend's neck was fifty or sixty centimetres long. From the top of the neck, Noah's head smiled broadly. He lifted the little plastic bag up to shoulder-height, and suddenly the goldfish became the size of a small shark.

'Just when you thought it was safe to go back to the fairground ...' Noah joked, turning the bag so it looked as if the giant fish were about to swim straight for Rex.

A movement behind Noah's narrow neck caught Rex's eye. He turned to see what it was, but there was nothing behind him but shadows and mirrors. He shook his head. There were only the three of them in the mirror room. He must have just caught a glimpse of his own reflection or something.

'This one makes me look three metres tall,' Bobo said, admiring himself in a different mirror.

'This one makes my legs bend backwards,' Noah laughed, looking at himself in another.

Rex moved to yet another mirror and peered into it. His jaw dropped open in amazement. This mirror was the best one yet.

'Whoa,' he cried. 'This one makes it look like Biowulf's standing right behind me!'

A blast of warm breath hit Rex on the back of the neck. He let out a low groan. 'Biowulf's standing behind me, isn't he?'

Noah looked at his friend, then he looked at the hulking wolf-like Evo standing behind him. 'Yeah,' he squeaked. '*Right* behind you.'

Rex spun on the spot and came face to muzzle with Biowulf. 'You mind stepping back a little there?' he asked, covering his mouth and nose with his hand. 'Your breath is kinda ripe.'

Biowulf bared his teeth and let out a low, threatening growl. 'Don't push me, runt,' he snarled.

'Seriously, dude,' Rex coughed. 'Have a breath mint.'

Biowulf's arms twitched. His clawed fingers bunched into fists. He was about to lunge when a voice stopped him.

'That's enough, Biowulf.'

A man in a long, flowing coat stepped from the shadows. His long black hair hung down by his face, the streak of white clearly visible in the half-darkness.

'Van Kleiss,' Rex spat.

'I didn't realise this fairground had a freak show,' Bobo sneered.

Van Kleiss fixed Bobo with a withering look. 'Cheeky monkey,' he said, dryly.

Two more shapes emerged from behind mirrors. Their warped reflections looked no stranger than the figures themselves. One was a giant lizard-like creature, with crystals growing from his shoulder and the end of one arm. The other was a girl. Her greasy black hair hung down over her face, hiding it from view. A pair of thick, muscular arms drooped from her sagging shoulders. Below those, sticking out from her ribcage, were another pair of much smaller arms.

'Skalamander and Breach,' Noah gasped.

'The gang's all here,' Rex added. 'What do you want, Van Kleiss?'

'Ah, straight down to business, I see,' Van Kleiss said. 'Very well. I want your help, Rex.'

Rex snorted. 'You're kidding, right?'

'As you know, Rex, away from the soil of Abysus, I am weakened. All I ask is that you let me absorb just a few of your nanites, to help build up my strength a little.' He smiled, showing all his teeth. 'So that I may enjoy the fairground freely.'

'Hey, guys,' Rex said, talking to his friends, but not taking his eyes off Van Kleiss. 'My arch-enemy wants me to help make him stronger. What do you think?'

Bobo cracked his knuckles. 'I think we should kick his sorry butt all the way back to Abysus.'

'Sorry,' Rex said, with a shrug. 'The monkey has spoken.'

As Rex's shoulders raised into the shrug, the Smackhands appeared around his arms. He brought them up sharply, slamming them into Biowulf's chin. The Evo henchman was sent hurtling backwards across the room. His reflection bounced back at him from a dozen distorted mirrors, before he *crunched* down onto the ground.

Bobo whipped out his twin pistols and sprayed laser blasts towards Van Kleiss and Breach. They ducked for cover behind a mirror. The blasts bounced off the reflective surfaces and ricocheted around the room, forcing the heroes to dodge and weave.

'OK,' Bobo muttered, slipping the guns back into his belt. 'Bad idea.'

Skalamander crashed across the room and swung wildly at Noah with his crystal club arm.

'The fish,' Noah yelped, as he ducked beneath the arm. 'Watch the goldfish!' He fired a kick into Skalamander's lower back. It didn't hurt the enormous Evo, but it threw him off balance. He staggered forwards. Bobo raced up Skalamander's scaly back and drove both feet against the back of his head. The henchman hit the ground, face-first.

'Who's next?' Rex asked, raising the Smackhands.

'Breach, take us back to Abysus,' Van Kleiss hissed. '*Now!*'

Silently, Breach conjured up one of her swirling red portals that would allow Van Kleiss and the rest of The Pack to teleport home. Van Kleiss took a step towards the portal, but something pulled him back.

He turned and saw the portal's distorted reflection in the closest mirror. A wind seemed to whip out from within the reflected portal. But this wind wasn't blowing out, it was sucking in!

Van Kleiss felt his feet slide across the floor

towards the mirror. 'Breach?' he demanded. 'What's happening?'

There was a series of sharp cries, as everyone in the room started sliding towards the portal in the mirror. Van Kleiss was pulled in first, passing right through the glass as if it didn't exist.

Biowulf's claws scraped across the floor, but he couldn't hold on. He went next, closely followed by the flailing Skalamander.

Noah and Bobo were holding onto a mirror's frame. Their legs were pulled out behind them as the force of the wind became greater and greater.

With a cry of shock, their grips slipped and they went tumbling through the air, towards the mirror portal. A split-second before they were sucked through, Rex caught their arms. He was standing his ground, his Punk Buster legs braced against the wind.

He yanked his friends clear just as Breach went spinning past. As she was sucked into the portal, the wind dropped, and silence returned to the room.

'What was *that*?' Rex asked. The portal Breach had made was gone, but its warped reflection was still there in the mirror.

Noah had managed to keep hold of his plastic bag throughout his whole ordeal. He held it up and looked inside, checking his fish was still OK. It swum around happily.

'I don't know what that was, kid,' Bobo shrugged. He raised a hand and pointed to the mirror portal. Something moved within it. 'And I don't know what *that* is, either.'

CHAPTER 4

'STAND BACK,' Rex warned. All three of them took a step away from the mirror. Rex brought out his Smackhands. Bobo clenched his hairy fists. Noah shielded the goldfish.

A man in a neat white suit slid out through the surface of the mirror. He landed smoothly on his feet, right in front of the startled heroes. His hair was short and neat, the colour of his suit, but with a single black stripe running through it.

Strangest of all, on his left hand the man wore a bright yellow foam finger. The phrase "You're #1" was printed on it in red lettering.

'That was ... *interesting*,' the man said. He spotted Rex and the others and his face lit up in a warm smile. 'Hello there,' he said. He reached out to shake Rex's hand, realised they were far too large to shake, so changed direction and caught hold of Noah's hand instead. He pumped it up and down, like he was jacking up a car. 'Dan Nice. Wonderful to meet you.'

'Uh ... hi,' said Noah.

Dan pointed with his foam finger. 'Loving the fish.'

'Thanks,' Noah muttered, but Dan was already crouching down beside Bobo.

'And who do we have here?' he asked. He reached out with his normal hand to give Bobo a playful pat on the cheek.

'Come any closer with that hand and I'll make you eat it, bub.'

Dan's eyes went wide. 'You can *talk*!' he exclaimed. 'That's incredible. Such intelligence. And, may I say, that's a fetching hat you're wearing!'

Bobo grunted, but didn't reply. Dan was already straightening up and turning back to Rex. The newcomer opened his mouth to speak, but a sudden movement from within the mirror cut him off.

A blonde-haired girl in a frilly pink dress slid from the reflected portal. Her matching pink high-heeled shoes *clopped* noisily on the floor as she jumped up and down with excitement.

'Like, OMG!' she shrieked. 'That was just, like, the most awesome thing *ever*. I mean, like, *whoa*!'

She looked around at the room, her dress twirling around her as she turned. She clamped her hands on either side of her face, trying to hold in her excitement. Her gaze finally found Rex. She skipped over and threw her arms around him.

'OMG!' she cried. 'You have, like, the biggest mechanical hands I've ever seen. I mean, I've never seen any other mechanical hands before, but if I had, yours would be the biggest by, like, far.'

'Who *are* you?' Rex asked, when the girl finally pulled away.

'Name's Sealina,' she said. 'Although, most of my friends call me "Seal".'

'Seal?' Rex frowned.

'OMG, I, like, totally love the way you say my name! It's so *cute*.'

Rex turned to the sharply-dressed man. 'And *Dan Nice*?'

'That's me,' Dan said, flashing his winning smile.

'What's with the foam finger?' Rex asked.

'Ah, yes, a rather unfortunate affliction,' Dan said. 'Still, one learns to adjust,' he added, brightly.

'Wait, that thing's your actual hand?' Noah asked.

Dan held up the hand and made the finger waggle up and down. 'All me!' he chirped.

'White hair, black streak,' Rex muttered. 'Foam finger in place of metal glove. *Dan Nice. Van Kleiss.*'

'Kid, you're talking to yourself again,' Bobo told him.

'You're a mirror image,' Rex realised with a start. 'You're like a mirror version of Van Kleiss.'

'So Van Kleiss becomes Dan Nice,' Noah said. 'And Breach becomes Seal!'

'What, she's going to start balancing balls on her nose now?' Bobo asked. 'This I gotta see.'

'Not *that* kind of seal,' Noah told him.

'But wait,' Rex said. 'Biowulf and Skalamander went into the mirror, too. Where are their –'

THUD.

Two small shapes slid from within the mirror, just as the portal closed. They landed in a tangled pile at Rex's feet. Rex looked down into the trusting brown eyes of a Labrador puppy. It wagged its tail, then noisily licked his shoe.

Beside the dog, a chameleon-like lizard turned the colour of the floor and eyed the group suspiciously.

'You have *got* to be kidding me,' Rex said.

Noah thrust the goldfish bag into Bobo's hand and snatched up the dog. Its tiny tongue lapped at his face, making him laugh. 'Can we keep him?' Noah asked. 'I'll call him Biowoof. I'll take him for walks every day. It'll be awesome.'

'OMG, he, like, totally loves you, you can so tell,' Seal babbled.

The chameleon crawled up Noah's back and perched on his shoulder. It settled there, but looked ready to move away at any moment.

'You have a real way with animals,' Dan told him. 'It's wonderful to see.'

Noah blushed. 'Thanks.'

'You can't keep them, they might be dangerous,' Rex said. 'They might *all* be dangerous,' he added, more quietly.

'Come on, you said yourself they're the opposite of The Pack,' Noah whispered. 'So they're the *opposite* of dangerous.'

Rex thought about this. It did seem to make sense. Besides, he couldn't just leave the Mirror Pack to roam around. There was only one thing for it.

'*Yeeeeeeeha!*' Rex cried. A few metres behind him, sitting in the roller-coaster cars, Noah, Bobo and their new friends laughed and shrieked with excitement.

Dan Nice, it had turned out, had some sort of control over non-organic materials. He couldn't control plants like Van Kleiss could, but he *was* able to bend the broken track back into place.

The motor that powered the whole roller-coaster was still broken, but that didn't matter. Rex had just the solution.

The Rex Ride zoomed up a steep slope in the track, towing the coaster cars along with it. Everyone raised their hands above their heads as they went into a loop-the-loop. Everyone except Noah, that is, who was clinging tightly to Biowoof, his goldfish and the lizard, whom he had named Mandy. He screamed and laughed along with the others, though, enjoying every moment of the ride.

A *buzz* in Rex's pocket alerted him that his phone was ringing. Keeping one hand on the Rex Ride's handlebars, he pulled out the phone. He groaned when he read the caller display.

'Hey, Six,' he said, holding the phone to his ear. 'Kinda busy right now.'

'Is that screaming I hear?' Six demanded.

'Yeah, but it's good screaming. Not Evos-coming-to-kill-everyone screaming.'

'I'm calling curfew,' Six told him. 'Get back to base.'

'But, Six, we were just —'

'Curfew,' Six repeated. '*Now.*'

CHAPTER 5

THEY STEPPED DOWN FROM THE ROLLER-COASTER, all still buzzing with the sheer excitement of it. Seal threw her arms around Rex's neck for a second time and hugged him tightly.

'Like, *wow*, OK?' she gushed. 'Just ... just *wow*. That was, like, *so* amazing! I mean, we were all *waaaah*! And you were, like, *zoooooom*! Awesome, just awesome!'

'It *was* pretty awesome,' Rex agreed. 'Shame it had to end so soon. I bet we could have really supercharged the Wheel of Terror.'

'We could always stick around,' Bobo suggested. 'I mean, it wouldn't exactly be the first time we'd ignored anything Six said.'

'It's tempting,' Rex said. 'But I guess we did kinda promise Six. Besides,' he added, turning to Seal and Dan Nice, 'he'll want to meet you guys.'

'I don't know who this "Six" is that you refer to,' Dan said, 'but I'm sure it will be an absolute joy to meet him.'

Bobo grunted. 'Man, are you in for a disappointment.'

'He won't care about these two,' Noah said, hopefully. He pointed down at Biowoof, who was running in circles around his feet, and then at Mandy, who was perched on his shoulder again. The lizard quietly licked her own eyeball. 'Will he?'

'I doubt it,' Rex shrugged. He reached down and scratched the dog behind the ears. 'Six isn't exactly what you'd call an animal lover.'

'Tell me about it,' muttered Bobo.

'So I can take them home?' Noah asked.

Rex couldn't see the harm in it. 'OK,' he said. 'Just keep an eye on them. Don't let them go running off or anything. The doc might want to check them out and make sure they've had their shots or whatever.'

He stopped patting Biowoof and stood up. The dog began pawing at Rex's leg, trying to get his attention again.

'Don't worry, I won't let them out of my sight!' Noah said. 'Here Biowoof,' he called, patting the front of his leg. The puppy glanced at him, then stared longingly up at Rex.

'Here, boy,' Noah urged, but the dog didn't budge. 'Come on, Biowoof. Who's a good doggy? Who's a good doggy? Doggy, doggy, doggy.'

Noah glanced up to find everyone looking back at him. He coughed below his breath, blushed, then bent down and picked the dog up. It whined and whimpered and squirmed in Noah's arms, as it struggled to be nearer Rex. Noah tickled the dog under the chin. It barked happily, then licked the end of Noah's nose.

'That's more like it,' Noah grinned. He nodded to the others. 'Well, I'll catch you guys later!'

'Farewell, my young friend,' said Dan, giving Noah a friendly wave of his foam finger. 'Safe journey.'

He kept waving until Noah was out of sight. 'What a nice young man,' he said, once Noah had gone. 'And I should know. It's like they say – Dan Nice knows nice!'

'Uh ... *who* says that?' Rex asked.

Dan laughed. 'No one,' he admitted, 'but I'm really hoping it'll catch on.'

'Good luck with that,' Rex said. 'OK, let's get back to base.'

He made for the fairground's exit. Seal wrapped

her arm around his and teetered alongside him in her high heels, chattering constantly. Dan walked on Rex's other side, whistling a bright, cheerful tune.

Still standing by the roller-coaster, Bobo looked down at the bag in his hand. A bulbous pair of eyes looked back at him, unblinking.

'Hey,' he said, calling after the others, 'how come I'm the one left holding the goldfish?'

CHAPTER 6

DAN STEPPED FORWARD, his normal hand outstretched. 'Dan Nice,' he beamed. 'It's a real pleasure to meet you, Mr Six. I've heard so much about you from Rex and Bobo.'

Agent Six regarded Dan with suspicion. He didn't shake his hand. 'Have you?' he asked 'Did they tell you what I do to non-authorised personnel who wander in to Providence Base?'

Dan's smile didn't falter. 'No, they did not,' he said, 'and I'm almost certain I don't want to find out.'

'He's with us, Six,' Rex said. He gestured to Seal, who was holding onto his arm with both hands now. 'And so's she.'

Dr Holiday nudged Six aside and shook Dan's hand. It went from being a greeting to being a physical examination in the space of half a second.

'Hi. Dr Holiday,' she said, before adding, 'Skin is a little dry, but otherwise fine. Body temperature feels normal.'

Dan waited patiently until she had finished prodding at his hand. 'Thank you for that vote of confidence, Dr Holiday,' Dan said, with a wink. 'As far as I'm aware, I'm in good health, but it's always nice to have a second opinion.'

Holiday turned to Rex. 'And you're saying the mirror just ... spat them out?'

'Yeah. No. Kind of,' Rex said. 'Breach made a portal between the mirrors, and then the reflection of one of them sucked The Pack into it.'

'The reflection sucked them in?' Six asked. 'That's not possible.'

'Hey, I'm just telling you what I saw,' Rex protested. 'I leave the whole *is-it-or-isn't-it-possible* thing up to you guys.'

'The kid's telling it straight,' Bobo said. 'Van Kleiss and the rest of 'em got pulled right inside the mirror. Few seconds later, out pop these two.'

'Four went in and two came out?' Holiday asked.

'Uh, no, not exactly,' Rex said. 'There was a puppy and a lizard thing, too. Noah took them home to look after. I don't think they're Evo.'

'Let's hope not, for his sake,' Six said.

'I think the worst that could happen is the dog licks him to death,' Rex said. His brow furrowed. 'Which, come to think about it, would be a pretty horrible way to go.'

Six turned his attention to the girl at Rex's side. 'Who's your girlfriend?' he asked, prompting a high-pitched giggle from Seal.

'I'm Sealina,' she smiled. 'But like I said to Rex, all my friends, like, *totally* call me Seal.'

Six felt his eye twitch. 'Then I'll, like, totally call you Sealina,' he said.

'OMG, your dad's, like, such an old stiff,' Seal whispered. 'He totally needs to lighten up.'

'He's not my dad,' Rex objected.

'Wow,' Six said to Rex. 'And I thought *you* could be irritating. She's a whole new level.'

'But Rex is right,' Holiday said. She was leaning in, looking more closely at Seal's perfect blonde hair. 'She's the exact opposite of Breach. Not just the way she looks, but the way she behaves, too. She's ... peppy.'

'I don't do *peppy*,' Six said.

'You'd rather she was acting all sullen and attacking you with her super-strong arms?' Holiday asked.

Six didn't answer, but Rex had a sneaking suspicion that the answer to that question was probably "yes".

'We're going to have to ask you a few questions,' said Six, turning to Dan.

'I shall do my very best to answer them as openly as I possibly can,' Dan said, sincerely. 'Any friend of Rex and Bobo's is a friend of mine.'

'Where did you come from?' Six asked.

'From your point of view, I suppose we came from the Mirror World,' Dan explained. 'It's sort of a parallel universe to this one, similar in many ways, but very different in others.'

'Examples?' Six said.

'Well, take the nanite accident,' Dan continued. 'Rex tells me that here the nanites cause untold damage, turning many of those affected into rampaging monsters.'

'That's right,' Holiday confirmed. 'So?'

'Back in our world, the accident was a blessing. There were one or two ... unfortunate abnormalities, yes.' He held up his foam finger hand. 'But, by and large, those affected became better than they were before. Like young Rex here, or Bobo.'

Six glanced down at the chimp. He paused for a moment, caught off-guard, before asking, 'Why are you holding a fish?'

'Long story,' Bobo replied.

'What's the last thing you remember before you came through the mirror?' Holiday asked.

'I can't speak for Seal here, but I was attending a charity fundraiser,' said Dan. He smiled. 'One does what one can for the less advantaged.'

'Just answer the question,' said Six.

'Yes, sorry,' Dan said. 'I had just handed over my donation, when a circle of red light appeared in front of me. Before I could react, it had pulled me through.'

'What about you, Goldilocks?' Six asked. 'What happened to you?'

'Well, I was on the phone to Tina, talking about how Suzanne and Corey just, like, bailed from Sam's birthday party last night, and I was all, like, "It's a total scandal," and she was, like, "I know!" and I was all, like, "Tell me about it".'

'I think what Mr Six is asking, Seal, dear, is, what happened in the immediate moment before you arrived at the fairground?' said Dan.

'Oh,' said Seal. 'What you said. Red circle. Pulled inside. *Blah, blah, blah.*'

'Thank you, Mr Nice,' Holiday said. 'Six hasn't really mastered talking to teenagers.'

'Please, call me Dan.' He took Holiday's hand and kissed it lightly. 'And I'm delighted to assist you in any way I can.'

'An' I thought that guy couldn't get any smarmier,' Bobo muttered, pulling a disgusted face.

Six stepped between Holiday and Dan, splitting them up. 'You can *assist* me in the interview room. There's a lot more I'd like you to explain.'

'Want me to come?' Seal asked.

'No,' said Six, firmly. '*Definitely* not. Go with Rex. He'll help you get settled in until we figure out what to do with you. You can stay in the room next to his.'

'OMG, you hear that?' Seal chirped. She tightened her grip on Rex's arm. 'We're going to be, like, *neighbours!*'

Rex forced a smile. 'Yay,' he said, quietly. 'I, like, *totally* can't wait.'

CHAPTER 7

NEXT MORNING, REX ROLLED OUT OF BED, wiping the crusts of sleep from his eyes. He yawned, stretched, thought about going back to sleep, then finally stood up.

It had taken a little longer than he'd expected to get Seal settled in. He'd shown her the room next to his, and Providence Agents had brought blankets and pillows for the bed. They'd also given her a TV, DVD player, games console and books to try to keep her occupied. None of it had worked.

The knocking had started on Rex's door just two minutes after he got back to his room. He opened the door to find Seal grinning back at him. She'd asked him how he was doing. He had told her he was fine.

She'd asked what his favourite colour was.

He'd said he didn't know.

She'd asked if he'd wanted to hang out.

He'd said it was really late, and that they should both be going to sleep.

She took the hint then, and slunk off back to her room. One minute and seventeen seconds later, there was another knock at the door, followed by another barrage of questions from the blonde-haired girl.

The knocking and the questions finally stopped around four o'clock in the morning. Rex had tried to sleep then, but he kept expecting another knock at the door, so he hadn't been able to settle properly.

It was nine o'clock now, and Rex felt as if he'd been punched in the head by an angry Evo. His eyes felt puffy and his mouth was dry. He staggered and felt his way around the room until he found his mobile phone. Hopefully Noah was finding his half of the Mirror Pack easier to deal with.

'Hello?' Noah sounded out of breath.

'Hey, Noah. What's happening?'

'I can't find Mandy,' Noah told him. 'She ... he ... *it* ... whatever, keeps changing colour to match the walls. One minute she's there, next minute, *poof*, gone.'

'That sounds bad,' Rex said.

'Bad, are you kidding? It's like the best game of hide-and-seek ever.'

'Oh. Cool,' replied Rex. 'How's the mutt doing?'

'Biowoof? He's doing great. He, uh, pees on the carpet a little bit more than I expected, but I figure he'll grow out of that.'

'Don't count on it,' Rex said. 'Just look at Bobo.'

'True,' Noah said. 'But a damp carpet's still a whole lot better than dealing with Biowulf and the rest of The Pack.'

'No arguments from me,' Rex said.

'You think we've seen the last of Van Kleiss?'

'Don't ask me,' Rex said. 'But as swaps go, right now I'd say we've definitely got the better side of the deal.'

The friends chatted for a while longer, then said their goodbyes. Rex yawned and stretched again and set about getting dressed. If he could get out of his room quickly enough, maybe there was a chance he could get some time to himself before Seal clamped onto him again.

But he wasn't going to count on it.

Rex stood in the Petting Zoo, with Dr Holiday and Agent Six by his side. Amazingly, he had managed to get out of the room without Seal spotting him. As he made his way to breakfast, though, Six had intercepted him and led him down to the Zoo. Rex could feel his stomach rumbling as he watched Dan Nice approach a savage Evo animal.

The creature looked like a sabre-toothed tiger that had somehow become merged with custard. It had the body of a big cat, but its skin hung down in gloopy strands from its back. It oozed down onto the grassy floor of the Petting Zoo, and formed a pool at the animal's feet.

'What's he doing?' Rex asked. 'That thing can get pretty wild.'

'He's trying to cure it,' Holiday explained, keeping her voice low so as not to startle the creature. 'He says he can absorb its nanites.'

'Can't be done,' Rex said. 'I tried, remember? This one's an Incurable.'

'We'll see,' said Six.

All three of them watched on as Dan laid his hands – the flesh one and the foam one – on the Evo's head. The animal tensed and let out a low, menacing snarl, but it didn't pull back. There was a sound, like the chirping of a thousand insects, and then —

WHOOSH!

The Evo transformed in a flash. One moment it was a custard-cat, the next, it was just a cat. It *miaowed* softly, rubbed its nose against Dan's human hand, then jumped up into his arms.

'Did you see that?' Holiday cried. 'That was incredible!'

'Impressive,' said Six, grudgingly.

'Thank you, Doctor, Mr Six,' Dan smiled. 'It was my pleasure.'

'Yeah, I could probably have done that,' Rex said under his breath, 'eventually.'

'I have absolutely no doubt about it, young Rex,' Dan said. 'I have no doubt whatsoever that you could. I just thought I'd do what I could to lighten your load. I hope you don't mind.'

'Uh, no,' Rex replied. 'You go right ahead, lightening the load or, or, whatever.'

Dan flashed him a grateful smile, then went back to playing with the cat.

'You checked in on Seal this morning?' Six asked.

Rex shook his head. 'Not yet.'

'Well,' said Six, raising an eyebrow, 'no time like the present.'

Rex paused outside the door to Seal's room, his hand raised and ready to knock. He felt bad. The girl was nice, and she was friendly, and he had no reason to dislike her. It was just the way she kept going on and on and didn't leave him alone that was starting to bother him. And now, here he was, about to knock on her door and make it all start over again.

'Hey, what ya doin'?' asked Bobo, shuffling along the corridor.

'Checking on Seal,' Rex sighed. 'Dan Nice is down in the Petting Zoo.'

'They've locked him up down there?' Bobo asked. 'I mean, the guy's a slimeball, but even he don't deserve the Petting Zoo.'

'He's not locked up, he's curing the Evos,' Rex explained. 'Even the incurable ones,' he added, quietly.

'Ain't that *your* job?'

Rex faked a smile. 'He's just helping out, that's all.'

Bobo shook his head. 'I don't trust him. Or any

of them. There's somethin' fishy about them. It's like they say, if somethin's too good to be true, then it probably is.'

'Give me these guys over the real Pack any day,' Rex replied. 'They don't worry me nearly as much.' He knocked on the door and was surprised when it swung open.

The room was in near darkness. Rex stepped inside, with Bobo at his heels. It took a moment for their eyes to adjust to the gloom; then they saw Seal.

She was sitting on the end of her bed, her knees up to her chest, her arms wrapped around them. Her hair, which had looked so neat and tidy yesterday, now hung down over her face like a curtain.

'Seal?' Rex asked, as he slowly approached the girl. She didn't reply, and it was clear that there was something very, very wrong.

'They don't worry you, huh, kid?' Bobo snorted. 'Maybe now's a good time to start.'

CHAPTER 8

VAN KLEISS STARED at his reflection in a mirror, and the reflection stared back. He reached up with his golden claw and pressed it against the one his mirror image wore. The glass was solid. There was no way through without breaking it.

On his left and right, Biowulf and Skalamander were tapping more mirrors, checking for portals hidden within the shiny surfaces. The area they were in was almost completely dark, but the thousands of mirrored surfaces that filled the space seemed to give off their own faint glow. It was enough that they could see their reflections in the glass, but no more.

KRICK.

Another mirror cracked at Skalamander's touch. It was the fifteenth one in as many minutes. This time Van Kleiss only barely managed to contain his temper.

'Be careful,' he warned. 'Any one of these could lead back to Earth. Break that one and we could be stuck here forever in ... in ... wherever it is we are.'

'Yeah, Skally, you're such a klutz sometimes,' said Breach.

The others turned to look at her, stunned into silence for just a moment. It was Van Kleiss who finally spoke. 'What did you say?' he asked.

Breach brushed her hair back over her ears. 'Just, like, how Skalamander's always breaking stuff. Like you said.'

Biowulf eyed her suspiciously. 'Why are you talking? You don't usually talk. Not like that, at least.'

Breach shrugged with all four of her arms. 'Maybe I just, like, never had anything to say to you guys before,' she said. 'I mean, it's not like we've exactly got much in common, right?'

Van Kleiss stroked his chin, deep in thought. 'An interesting development,' he said. 'Breach's entire personality seems to be altering.'

'It's like she's becoming the opposite of how she was,' Biowulf agreed.

'Yes, an opposite,' Van Kleiss realised. 'A *mirror image*, you might say.'

'Ew, check out my hair,' Breach whined. 'It's totally rank. Does anyone have, like, a gallon of shampoo?'

'She was less tiring before,' Biowulf growled. 'Let me shut her up.'

'Not yet,' Van Kleiss told him. 'Breach, come here.'

Breach stopped fiddling with her hair and strolled over. 'Dude, can I just say, I love that jacket?' she said. 'I've wanted to say that for a while, but you know, the whole being-quiet thing meant I couldn't. But I'm totally over that now, and that jacket is —'

'Silence,' Van Kleiss seethed. 'Just because you haven't spoken in a while, doesn't mean you have to make up for it now.'

'No, but I was just —'

'Ah!' Van Kleiss snapped.

'Yeah, but I was going to say —'

'*Ah!*' He mimed holding his mouth closed.

There was a pause. Breach bit her lip, as if trying to hold her own mouth closed. She couldn't contain herself for long.

'I meant —'

'*Silence!*' Van Kleiss roared. The word seemed to reflect around the vast space, bouncing off every mirror. That did the trick. Finally, Breach stopped talking. 'Now,' Van Kleiss said, taking a breath to help him contain his temper. 'I want you to try getting us out of here. Make another portal.'

'I tried when we got here,' Breach muttered. 'Total washout, remember?'

'Then try again,' Van Kleiss hissed. 'If at first you don't succeed ...'

Breach sighed loudly. 'Whatever,' she said, but she did as she was told. As she raised her arms, a shimmering circle of red light began to appear in front of her.

'That's it,' Van Kleiss said, as encouragingly as he could. 'It's working. Keep going.'

But even as the villain spoke, the portal started to change shape. It stretched and wobbled in the air. The round outline stretched at the top, becoming egg-shaped. Then the bottom began to fold upwards to the centre, even as the red glow fizzled out.

'No,' Van Kleiss roared. 'No, no, no!'

With a final *pop*, the portal vanished. Breach's arms fell to her sides.

'You idiot,' Van Kleiss spat. 'You're supposed to be able to make portals, that's what you do. That's your entire purpose!'

'Like, I tried to –'

'You *failed*, that's all that matters,' the villain roared. 'If you can't produce a portal when we need a portal, then tell me, Breach, what good are you?'

Breach didn't answer. Suddenly, she didn't feel like speaking. Her shoulders slumped and her hair fell down over her eyes. Silently, she went back to checking the mirrors, hoping that one of them would lead the way back home.

CHAPTER 9

R EX STOOD AT THE BACK of the room, watching nervously as Dr Holiday examined Seal. The girl was still sitting with her head hung down, but in the last few seconds she had pushed her hair back over her ears. That was a start, at least.

'Seal, can you hear me?' Holiday asked. 'Rex is worried about you. He thinks you might be ... having problems. Are you having problems, Seal?'

The girl slowly raised her eyes until they met Dr Holiday's. Then she nodded her head, just once.

'What sort of problems are you having?' Holiday asked, kindly. 'Maybe I can help.'

This was why he liked the doc, Rex thought. She was smart, funny, and she knew what to do in an emergency. And she looked *great* in those boots.

Seal's lips moved silently. Holiday leaned in closer. 'What did you say?' she asked.

'I d-don't know,' Seal whispered. 'I feel strange.'

'That's OK,' said Holiday, brightly. 'We're pretty

used to strange around here, aren't we, Rex?'

'We're all about strange here,' Rex replied. 'Hey, for all I know, Strange is my middle name.'

Seal looked up at him. A smile tugged at the corners of her mouth.

Breach's mouth pulled down into a miserable sneer. She was feeling worse with every second that passed. Van Kleiss was still furious at her, and Biowulf and Skalamander weren't paying her any attention.

For a few moments she had felt something she had never felt in her life before. She had felt ... happy, as if some great weight had been lifted from her shoulders.

But now the weight was back, and it was gradually getting heavier.

Seal felt her mood lightening. Dr Holiday was easy to talk to, and Rex was just, like, totally awesome!

The sadness she had felt had come on suddenly. It had overwhelmed her in the night, making her feel as if everything was a pointless waste of time, and that everyone in the world hated and despised her. She had never felt that way before, and she really hoped she never would again.

'Mandy? Mandy, where are you?' asked Noah, as he searched his kitchen for the chameleon. He was sure he'd seen it sneak in there, but now it was nowhere to be –

'No, don't eat the coffee!' Noah cried, as he finally spotted the lizard. It was standing on the kitchen counter, using its long tongue to lick coffee granules from inside a jar. The jar had been full just a few minutes ago. Now, it was almost completely empty.

Mandy's already bulging eyes seemed to bulge wider. The chameleon's colour went from pale blue to bright yellow, then cycled through red, orange, purple and half a dozen other colours Noah couldn't even name.

With a sudden *boing*, the lizard leapt up onto her feet. She scrabbled down onto the kitchen floor and began running in circles, around and around and around.

'Oh, great,' Noah groaned. 'A lizard on a caffeine rush. Just what I need!'

A short, sudden sound made Van Kleiss pause, his hand pressed against yet another mirror. He listened until the sound came again – a deep, snuffling snore from somewhere behind him.

Van Kleiss turned and scowled through the gloom. There, resting against a mirror, was Skalamander. His yellow eyes were closed over and there was even more drool than usual around his twisted mouth.

Asleep. He was asleep on the job!

A red mist of rage descended behind Van Kleiss' eyes. He stomped across to the snoring Skalamander and kicked him hard in the ribs. The lizard-like Evo opened his eyes and sat up with a start.

'I'm aware that you need your beauty sleep,' Van Kleiss growled. 'But trust me, now is *not* a good time!'

Skalamander looked around, as if trying to figure out what had just happened. This only made Van Kleiss more angry.

'Get *up*,' he seethed. 'Get up and *get searching*!'

Skalamander clambered quickly to his feet and shambled over to the closest mirror, working as fast as he could.

A whole world away, back at Noah's, Mandy was gradually slowing to a stop. She completed a few more circuits of the kitchen floor, before slouching down beneath the table and turning the colour of the lino.

'No more coffee for you,' Noah said. He stepped back and felt something squash beneath his heel. Biowoof let out a yelp of pain and shock, and Noah leapt like he'd been electrocuted.

'Hey, sorry, sorry,' he said, turning to the dog and bending down. Biowoof bared his tiny teeth and began to bark and snap angrily, forcing Noah to pull his hand away.

'Whoa there, little guy,' he said. 'It was an accident, that's all!'

'You know,' said Biowulf, sidling up to Van Kleiss, 'it could be worse.'

Van Kleiss blinked, surprised by the statement. 'What?'

'This. Being trapped in a mirror dimension,' Biowulf said. 'It could be a lot worse.'

'How, pray tell, could it be worse?' Van Kleiss asked.

'We could be on our own. At least we've got each other for company,' the henchman said. His jaw twisted in a strange way, and it took a moment for Van Kleiss to realise what Biowulf was doing.

'Are you … *smiling*?' he asked.

Biowulf nodded enthusiastically. 'It's like they say: smile, and the world smiles with you. Cry, and you wet your face.'

Van Kleiss pinched the bridge of his nose. He couldn't believe this. Breach and Skalamander behaved strangely all the time, but he could always count on Biowulf to be, well, Biowulf. Not today, it seemed.

'We should have a singsong,' the wolf Evo suggested. He began waving his arms above his head. '*Weeeee've got each ooooother*,' he sang, before Van Kleiss' claw wrapped tightly around his throat.

'Get back to work,' Van Kleiss barked.

'And let's never speak of this moment again.'

Seal was looking almost like her old self again. She was chatting happily to Dr Holiday, and didn't notice Rex as he tiptoed towards the door.

Just as he reached the exit, Agent Six stepped in to block the way. 'There you are,' Six said. 'We've got a rampaging Evo in the heart of Chicago. Time to get to work.'

'All *right*,' Rex grinned. He was happy to get back into action. It was time he reminded Six and Holiday who the *real* hero was around here.

'You're not going alone,' Six said. 'You've got an assistant going with you.'

Rex frowned. 'An assistant?'

A white-haired head popped up from behind Six's back. It smiled broadly and gave Rex a friendly wink. 'Dan Nice, reporting for duty,' Dan said. He fired off a friendly salute. 'Let's go get 'em, kiddo!'

CHAPTER 10

THE KEEP, an enormous Providence aircraft capable of carrying tanks into battle, cruised above the Chicago skyline. It was headed for the downtown area of the city, where an Evo was running riot.

Rex stood by one of the Keep's bay doors, looking at the rooftops as they *swooshed* by below. Dan Nice stood beside him, grinning happily.

'This is going to be terrific,' he clapped. 'You and me, working together, side by side. We'll fix up this Evo in no time.'

'Yeah,' Rex said, without enthusiasm. 'It'll be great.'

'And think of the other Evos we can cure,' Dan Nice continued. 'Why, the two of us could probably fix every problematic Evo in the world!'

'That sounds like a whole lot of work,' Rex said.

'It would be,' Dan admitted, 'but we'd do it, because we'd be a team. An unstoppable team, Rex and Dan Nice – you'd be the leader, obviously. Rex and Dan Nice, curing the world, one Evo at a time!'

'I'd *so* be the leader,' Rex agreed, but deep down he was having doubts. Dan Nice had cured an Evo Rex had assumed was incurable. If that sort of thing continued, Rex had a niggling worry that he might suddenly find himself out of a job.

With a whine of engines, the Keep began to descend. Rex could just make out the shape of an Evo down on the ground. He looked almost normal, aside from his arms, which stretched out like tentacles. The tentacles cracked like whips as the man lashed them at the Evo Agents gathered around him.

'This should be a piece of cake,' Rex said.

The Keep was still twenty or more metres from the ground, but Rex didn't want to wait around any longer. Catching hold of Dan Nice beneath the arms, he stepped out of the aircraft and immediately activated his Boogie Pack.

The twin turbines flipped out from his shoulders, allowing Rex to swoop down and land on the ground near the Evo. Dan Nice rolled expertly on the tarmac, then bounced to his feet, ready for anything.

Well ... *almost* anything. As Dan caught sight of his reflection in a shop window, he froze. For a long moment he just stood there, his eyes fixed on his mirror image, his foam finger twitching nervously.

'Uh, are you OK?' Rex asked him. At the sound of his voice, the Evo turned and glared. Rex gave him a nod. 'With you in a minute,' he said.

Dan gave himself a shake, and drew his eyes away from the glass. 'I ... uh ... sorry about that,' he said, offering up a nervous smile. 'I guess I just ...'

His voice trailed off as he saw himself in another window. Dan's eyes slowly scanned around in a circle. Reflections of himself looked back at him from every store front.

The Evo took a step towards them, snapping both tentacles out with two loud *cracks*.

'*In a minute*,' Rex scowled. 'Kinda in the middle of something here!' He placed a hand on Dan's shoulder, only for Dan to pull away.

'Don't touch me!' Dan screeched. He turned and ran, staggering past the wreckage of cars and other vehicles damaged by the Evo.

'Wait, come back,' Rex called after him. The Evo let out an angry screech. 'Hold that thought,' Rex said. 'I'll get to your butt-kicking as soon as I can ...'

With that, he raced after Dan Nice. The Evo stood in the middle of the street, swaying slightly as it wondered what to do. Then, somewhere deep inside its deranged mind, it came to a decision. Coiling its whip-like arms tight by its sides, it hurried off in the direction Rex had run.

'N-n-no!' Dan was stammering when Rex finally found him. He was standing beside the Cloud Gate sculpture — a colossal piece of artwork that looked like a very shiny jelly bean. Dan was fixated on his reflection on the sculpture's surface. It was bent and twisted like the reflections in the Hall of Mirrors.

As Rex approached, Dan dropped to his knees and held his arms over his head. He screwed his eyes tightly closed and bent low, as if trying to hide from his own reflection.

'Uh, hey, Dan, are you OK?' Rex asked, approaching cautiously. A sob of anguish was Dan's only reply. 'I'm going to take that as a "no",' Rex decided. 'I think we should probably get you back to Providence Base. They should be able to —'

GRRRRRRRAHHHK!

Rex rolled his eyes. 'One second,' he said, then

he spun, transforming his arms into the powerful Smackhands.

'Trying to have a conversation here,' Rex said, as one of his machine fists crunched hard against the Evo, slamming it against the side of a car. The Evo let out a low groan, before slumping to the ground, unconscious.

'Sorry about that,' Rex said. He turned back to the spot where Dan had been, only to find it completely empty. Rex looked around him, but there was no sign of the man anywhere. From somewhere off in the distance, though, Rex heard his anguished screams.

'The whole losing the job thing?' he said to himself. 'Suddenly, I'm feeling a lot more confident.'

He looked down at the sleeping Evo and his Smackhands returned to normal. He placed one hand on each of the monster's motionless tentacles.

'I'd tell you to try to relax, but it looks like you beat me to it,' Rex said. 'Now, don't worry, this isn't going to hurt a bit.'

CHAPTER 11

REX STRETCHED OUT A HAND and helped up the fallen man. Two Providence Agents raced over and quickly wrapped a blanket around the man's shoulders.

'Wh-what happened?' he stammered.

'Nothing for you to worry about,' Rex told him. 'You just kinda turned into a monster for a while there and smashed a lot of stuff up.'

The man's mouth fell open. 'I ... I did?'

'It's over now, but you might have a rash for a day or two, where the tentacles were.'

'*Tentacles?*'

'And maybe some bruising. You know, from where I hit you with my giant hammer hand? Other than that, though, you'll be fine.' Rex thought for a moment. 'Just to be on the safe side, though, I'd avoid eating squid for a while,' he added.

As the Agents led the man away, there was a brief hiss of static in Rex's ear, and he knew Six was about to speak to him over his communicator. He decided to beat him to it.

'So ... Dan Nice kinda freaked out,' Rex said.

'I saw that,' Six said. 'I was watching it on screen.'

'Pretty freaky, huh?' Rex said. 'I mean, even by our standards.'

'Pretty freaky,' Six agreed. 'You should keep a close eye on him.'

'I would, if I had any idea where he was,' Rex replied. 'I suppose I could pop out the Boogie Pack and have a scout around.'

'No need,' said Six. 'I've got Agents closing on him now. He's just lying in the road, so I doubt he'll be too much trouble to contain. Head back to the Keep and they'll meet you with him there,' Six instructed. 'When you're both on board he's your responsibility until you get back here. Understood?'

Rex understood, but he didn't like it. 'Why is he my responsibility? I didn't even want him tagging along!'

'He's your responsibility because I say he is,' Six snapped. 'And because, if he really starts to lose it, you might be the only one who can stop him.'

'Thanks for that happy thought,' Rex said, and he made his way back to the Keep.

Rex was leaning back in his seat when Dan Nice was led through the bay doors of the Keep, an Agent on each side of him. The Agents had their arms through his and were half-dragging, half-carrying him along.

Dan's eyes were panicked and wide. They flitted nervously around the inside of the Keep as he was brought on board and dumped onto a chair. He sat there with his head low, mumbling below his breath.

'Hey, Dan,' greeted Rex. 'Feeling better?'

Dan's head twitched violently and he almost choked on a sob.

'Guess not,' Rex said.

There was a crackle in his ear. 'He on board yet?' Six asked.

'Just got on,' Rex replied, keeping his voice low so Dan couldn't hear. 'He still looks pretty freaked out.'

'What's he doing?'

'Uh, just kind of, muttering to himself and

looking like a maniac.' Rex blew out his cheeks. 'I guess you didn't see this one coming, huh?'

'Yes,' said Six. 'I did.'

Rex sat forward in his seat. 'You did?' he yelped. Then, more quietly, 'You did? Then why did you send him out?'

'I had to test my theory,' Six said. 'Besides, all that brave and dashing hero stuff can really get on your nerves after a while.'

'Hey! I'm a brave and dashing hero,' Rex protested weakly.

There was a pause. 'Yeah, kid. Keep telling yourself that,' Six said. 'I knew Nice had to be too good to be true. No one can be that perfect all the time. Except for me.'

'So you thought you'd let him tag along with me in the hope he went into meltdown?' Rex snapped.

'Come on, kid, I knew you could handle him,' Six said. 'Consider it a compliment.'

'You know, Six, sometimes I really don't think I like you,' Rex sighed.

Rex could almost hear the satisfied smirk in Six's voice. 'Guess that means I'm doing my job.'

There was a roar of engines and the Keep lifted straight up into the air. The Agents who had brought Dan on board were strapped into seats on either side of him, making sure he didn't bolt for the door.

'Remember, Rex, he's your responsibility until you're back here,' Six reminded him. 'Keep him out of trouble.'

'I'll see what I can do,' Rex replied, and the line went dead.

The Keep was cruising across the city, gradually getting higher as the pilot set a course for Providence HQ. Rex had just begun to think about getting some shut-eye, when Dan Nice began to speak.

'R-Rex,' he wheezed. 'Help me.'

Unclipping his safety harness, Rex got to his feet and hurried over to where Dan was sitting. Up close, he could see that Dan's skin was deathly pale, and his whole body was vibrating.

'What's up?' Rex asked. 'What do you need?'

'N-nanites. So ... weak. Need to absorb n-nanites.'

Rex had heard that one before. Maybe Dan Nice and Van Kleiss weren't so different, after all. The difference was, Van Kleiss was a villain, and Dan – as far as Rex could tell – was one of the good guys.

'OK,' Rex sighed. He crouched down in front of the man. 'How do you want to do this?'

CHAPTER 12

'**Y**OU SHOULD REST,' said Biowulf, but Van Kleiss was not ready to rest.

'You should mind your own business,' he snapped, as he checked the surface of another mirror.

Van Kleiss would never admit it, but he *did* need to rest. He had felt weak back on Earth, but here, in this Mirror Kingdom, his strength was fading even further.

But how could he rest when things were so bad? They had been searching for hours, with no sign of a way out. At least Biowulf had stopped acting so strangely, and was back to his usual snarling self. Breach and Skalamander hadn't displayed any more strange behaviour either, but it was probably only a matter of time before all four of them lost their minds.

He raised an arm to check the surface of another mirror, but found his muscles were too weak to lift it all the way. The arm swung back down to his side. His legs buckled, and Van Kleiss slumped down onto one knee. He wanted to fall further, wanted to collapse onto the ground and just lay there until he passed out. But he would not let The Pack see him in that condition.

He gritted his teeth and sucked in a breath, trying to stop the world around him from spinning into blackness. He would not fall further. He would not.

'N-need nanites,' he uttered. 'Need nanites *now*.'

Dan Nice's human hand clamped onto Rex's arm.

'OK, take some, but not too many. Just take what you need so we can get you back to HQ. The doc should be able to fix you up then.'

'Th-thank you, Rex,' Dan said. He managed a faint smile, and then Rex felt a strange *whooshing* sensation inside him, as some of his nanites flowed from his body into Dan's.

Rex watched the man closely. As Dan absorbed the nanites, the colour began to return to his skin. The shaking, which had been making his whole body tremble, eased away.

'Hey, good news, I think it's working,' Rex told him. 'How do you feel?'

Dan's grip tightened around Rex's arm.

'Hey, loosen up there,' Rex told him. He tried to pull his arm away, but Dan had it held fast. 'OK, kinda starting to hurt now.'

'M-more,' Dan hissed, his eyes blazing wildly. 'Must have *more!*'

Van Kleiss stood up suddenly. The weakness that had brought him to his knees was fading. He could feel it slipping away, and his strength rushing back in to fill the void.

He couldn't explain it, but it felt like his body was being filled up with nanites, and with every second that passed he was becoming more powerful. A wicked grin crept across his face.

'More,' Van Kleiss hissed. 'Must have *more!*'

'Uh, guys, a little help here?' said Rex, looking to the two Agents sitting on either side of Dan.

Dan's hand was still clamped around Rex's forearm. No matter how hard he tried, Rex couldn't prise his fingers free. He could activate one of his machine forms, but he didn't want to hurt Dan if he could help it.

Rex felt his own strength begin to fade. Dan Nice's mouth was twisted into a wicked grin. He was looking more and more like Van Kleiss by the second, and Rex knew in that moment that Dan wouldn't stop until he had drained every single one of Rex's nanites.

The Agent on Dan's left reached over to try to stop him. The foam finger came up sharply and hit the Agent's face with a *doof.* The Agent slumped forward in his seat, out cold.

The other Agent made a grab for him, but Dan was too quick. He twisted sharply and raised his knee. It hit hard against the Agent's chin, sending him sprawling sideways.

'OK,' Rex said, 'I *was* worried about hurting you before. Now? Not so much.'

A flickering blue light spread across Rex's arms, right beneath Dan Nice's grip. Orange metal formed across the skin, as Rex brought out his Smackhands.

Dan let out a cry of pain and shock as the arm he was holding suddenly grew several times larger.

As the connection between them broke, the madness left Dan's eyes. He blinked and looked around, as if coming out of a deep trance. He seemed shocked by the unconscious Agents on either side of him.

'Rex?' he asked. 'Whatever's going on?'

'You know, Dan?' Rex replied, as the Smackhands retracted back into his arms. 'I was about to ask you that very same thing.'

Van Kleiss stood straight and tall. He flexed his muscles, then stretched and folded the fingers of his golden claw, as if testing them for the first time. The sensation of nanites flooding his body had stopped, but he felt strong now. Stronger than he had felt since leaving Abysus.

He couldn't explain what had happened, but that did not matter. All that mattered was that he was back to full power, and now nothing would stop him leading The Pack back to Earth.

'Biowulf, Breach, Skalamander,' he barked, pointing to each of them in turn. 'Double your efforts. Check every mirror. We're going to find the way out, and then Rex and his pathetic friends will pay dearly for what they have done!'

CHAPTER 13

EX LED DAN through the double doors of the Petting Zoo. Dan seemed to have returned to normal, but Rex wasn't taking any chances. He kept his distance, well outside of the mirror-man's reach.

'I really can't apologise enough,' Dan said. 'I don't know what came over me. It was totally out of character.'

'Yeah, so you've said,' Rex nodded. 'I'm sure it was nothing, but just in case, I want you to hang around here until I can get the doc to come check on you. You freaked out pretty majorly back there.'

Dan nodded, sadly. 'I did, didn't I?' He glanced around the Petting Zoo. 'What if the creatures attack?'

Rex shrugged. 'Cure them. Drain their nanites. You seem to be pretty good at that.'

Without another word, he stepped through the door and it swished closed, leaving Dan Nice all alone in the Petting Zoo.

Rex got in the elevator and pressed the button for

his floor. With any luck, Dr Holiday was still with Seal. He could tell her about Dan Nice, then head next door to bed. His head still felt woozy, and his body was still weakened. A rest, he guessed, would be just what the doctor would order.

The elevator didn't reach his floor. It stopped several floors below. The door swished open to reveal Agent Six standing there.

'Welcome back,' Six said. 'You look terrible. Come with me.'

Reluctantly, Rex followed Six out into a control room. Banks of video screens lined the walls. Servers and routers and other bits of computer equipment stood in racks between the monitors.

On the largest screen, at the far end of the room, a ghostly white face looked down. White Knight was the leader of Providence, and the only living thing on the planet not to be infected with nanites. He lived inside a sealed room, so the microscopic machines couldn't infiltrate his body. He was strict, stern and – Rex often thought – just a little creepy.

'Welcome back,' White Knight said.

'Yeah,' Rex muttered. 'Six said that already. Can we

get this over with? I'm kinda beat.'

'Quite,' White Knight said. 'We're worried about these ... newcomers,' he said. 'What happened on the mission today?'

'We got there, Dan saw his reflection, Dan went crazy, Dan ran away,' Rex explained. 'That's pretty much it.'

'The Evo,' White Knight began. 'You did cure the Evo, yes?'

Rex breathed on his fingernails and polished them against his shirt. 'I can't believe you're even asking me that question. Of course I cured the Evo. Piece of cake.'

'Two Agents came off the Keep on stretchers,' Six said. 'Why?'

'Yeah, Dan kinda freaked out again,' Rex said. 'I let him absorb a few of my nanites and –'

'You let him absorb your nanites?' Six growled. 'Why would you do that?'

'Because he looked sick, and you told me he was my responsibility,' Rex protested. 'I was worried he might die or something, and then you'd kill me.'

'What happened, *exactly*?' Six asked.

'He wouldn't let go,' Rex told them, 'just kept absorbing more and more. The Agents tried to stop him, but they didn't get very far. I had to pull out the Smackhands in the end just to get him to let go. After that, he calmed down, but I've put him in the Petting Zoo for now. Thought it'd keep him out of trouble.'

Six nodded. 'Good thinking.'

'Hey, did you just pay me a compliment?' Rex smirked.

'Don't get used to it.'

'I won't,' Rex said. 'Can I go rest up now? Are we done here?'

'Thank you, Rex, you're free to go,' White Knight said. 'Six and I will discuss what's to be done with Mr Nice.'

Rex nodded. 'Have fun with that,' he said, then he made his way back to the elevator and stepped inside. He jabbed the button for his floor and the lift trundled upwards until ...

PING!

The lift doors opened and Rex stepped out onto his corridor. It was only a few metres to Seal's room from where he was standing. The door was open, so he crept along and listened to the voices coming from within the room.

'OMG, your coat is to die for. You've got the whole, like, nerdy science-geek look totally nailed down. No offence. I totally meant that in a good way.'

'None taken.' That was Dr Holiday's voice, Rex realised. 'I'm glad you like my coat. Would you like to try it on?'

'Can I? That would be totally awesome!' Seal yelped. She was definitely sounding more like her old self, Rex thought. That was good news. Probably.

There was silence for a few seconds, while Dr Holiday took off her lab coat and Seal slipped it on. The quiet was shattered by Seal's squeal of delight. 'It's, like, a perfect fit,' Seal cried. 'OMG, how do I look? I bet I look awesome. Do I look awesome? Tell me I look awesome!'

'You look awesome,' Holiday said. 'There's a mirror over there. Take a look for yourself.'

Silence filled the room again. It lasted for several seconds.

'No, thanks,' Seal said, eventually.

'What? Why not?' Holiday laughed. 'What's the

point in trying on clothes if you don't get to see what they look like? Just take a look.'

'N-no,' Seal said. Rex recognised the tone in her voice. It was the same tone he had heard in Dan's voice, just before he'd flipped out and gone racing off across Chicago.

'Just take a look,' Holiday urged. 'It suits you.'

'Uh, Doc,' said Rex, stepping around the corner. Both women turned to look at him, startled by his sudden appearance. 'I'm really not sure that's such a good idea.'

CHAPTER 14

DR HOLIDAY CROSSED TO THE DOOR. 'Hey, this is girl-talk time,' she said, half-joking, half-stern. 'No boys allowed.'

Rex opened his mouth to explain, but Holiday hit the controls and the door closed between them, leaving Rex talking to solid metal.

He pressed his ear against the door, trying to listen for any clue as to what was happening inside. Dr Holiday's voice was muffled by the metal, but he could just make out what she was saying.

'See what I mean? It really suits you.'

There was a pause, during which Rex heard nothing but his own breath wheezing in and out. When Holiday finally spoke again, her voice was edged with panic. 'Seal? Seal, what's wrong? What's happening to your arms?'

A shriek of rage ripped out from within the room. Rex stepped back, just as two indents bent the metal of the door.

'Seal, calm down!' Holiday cried, before her voice was drowned out by the smashing of glass.

Rex had heard enough. Metallic feet grew from the end of his legs. He raised one Punk Buster and slammed it against the door. The metal crumpled inwards and Rex moved to enter the room.

A flailing shape exploded from inside and hit him hard on the chest. Seal thrashed and gnashed her teeth at him. Rex staggered as a powerful blow caught him across the cheek. Another hit him a half-second later, then another and another.

Rex put away the Punk Busters and brought out the Smackhands. He blocked Seal's attacks, caught her around the waist, then hurled her against the wall.

She hit the wall hard, but it didn't seem to slow her down. Twisting, she screeched angrily at Rex. Rex barely had time to realise the girl's slender arms had become thick and muscular, before she hurled herself at him again, battering against him with her freakishly large fists.

'What's with you guys and your mood swings?' Rex asked, as he batted Seal backwards along the corridor. She landed on all fours, poised like a sprinter at the start of a race. Rex braced himself as she launched forward, racing along the corridor towards him.

Just before she reached him, Rex swung with a metal fist. A swirling red circle appeared directly between them and Seal vanished inside it.

A moment later, Rex was thrown off balance, when Seal smashed into him from behind. He pulled in the Smackhands and rolled awkwardly when he hit the ground.

Rex turned to Holiday as she emerged from Seal's room. 'I didn't know she could make portals,' he said. 'Did *you* know she could make portals?'

Holiday shook her head. 'No, I didn't.'

'That's OK, then,' Rex said, relieved. 'I'd really hate to have been the only one who hadn't figured it out.'

Breach swung wildly with all four fists, driving them hard into Skalamander's stomach. The big lizard was taken by surprise. He bent double, winded by the sudden blow.

'Now what?' Van Kleiss said. He strode over to Breach, only for her to turn on him, her fists raised.

This surprised Van Kleiss. He hesitated, not sure how to deal with a Breach who was willing to stand up to him. He didn't take long to find his footing again.

'Stand down, Breach,' he told her. 'Or else you'll see first hand what my claw and I are capable of.'

WHUM!

Breach swung with both right arms. Van Kleiss ducked the more powerful punch, but was caught a glancing blow by the weaker lower arm.

Biowulf was on the girl in a heartbeat, holding her with his deadly claws, pinning her to the ground beneath the weight of his metallic body. 'What are you doing?' he snarled. 'Stop fighting before I beat the fight out of you for good.'

KA-RUNCH!

One of Breach's arms tore free and drove a bone-shattering uppercut into Biowulf's bottom jaw. The Evo was sent sprawling backwards and Breach sprang to her feet.

She looked around at the rest of The Pack, her eyes wide and staring behind her curtain of hair. The others hung back, none of them particularly keen on making the first move.

Breach turned in a slow circle, watching them all, ready to lash out. It wasn't until she caught sight of one of the mirrors that she stopped turning. As her eyes met those of her reflection, the rage inside her swelled. She lunged wildly for the mirror and threw her fists against the glass, shattering it into slivers.

With one hand she snatched up the wooden frame and hurled it at the next mirror. It punched through the reflective surface, smashing it instantly.

Breach spun around and saw that she was surrounded by hundreds of the mirrors – *thousands*, maybe. A voice in her head whispered to her.

Smash them, it told her. *Smash them all!*

Seal's fists slammed down on the floor where Rex had been just a half-second before. 'Smash you!' she growled. 'Smash you *all*!'

'You know,' said Rex, rolling to safety, 'I, like, *totally* prefer the old Seal.'

With a roar, the girl made to run at him, but Dr Holiday stepped into her path. With a jerk of one arm, Holiday stabbed a hypodermic needle into Seal's neck. The girl gave a low growl, which quickly became a groan. With a *thud* she toppled backwards onto the floor and lay there, snoring softly.

'Thanks, Doc,' Rex said. They looked down at the sleeping Seal as they got their breath back. 'Glad that's over. I've had enough excitement for one day.'

'Rex,' a voice hissed in his ear. He recognised it as Six straight away. 'We've got a problem. Dan Nice has broken out of the Petting Zoo. He's on a rampage through the lower floors, smashing every reflective surface he comes across.'

'Let me guess, you need someone to come down there and kick his butt?' Rex sighed.

'No, I can handle him,' Six said. 'I need you to help Noah.'

'Noah?' Rex frowned. 'What's up with Noah?'

'He's at the front door,' Six explained. 'Looks like he's having some kind of animal trouble.'

CHAPTER 15

NOAH HELD UP TWO BOXES, both made of a clear plastic material. Inside one, Biowoof hurled himself against the walls, barking and yelping and baring his jagged teeth in anger.

Inside the other, Rex saw nothing.

'Uh, aren't you missing something?' he asked, pointing to the empty box.

'No, Mandy's in there,' Noah said. 'But she keeps going completely invisible on me.'

Rex leaned in and peered into the box. 'You sure?' he asked. 'It looks pretty empty to me.'

Noah gave the box a shake. Something *clunked* noisily around inside it. Just for a moment, Rex thought he saw a shape flickering inside the box. It was big – much bigger than Mandy had been yesterday.

'Whoa, she's grown,' Rex said.

'Tell me about it,' Noah groaned. He looked completely exhausted. 'It took me two hours to cram her in that box. Meanwhile, I've got Biowoof trying to chew through the plastic and howling like a werewolf at the top of his voice the whole time.' He took a deep breath. 'I'm telling you, Rex, this being a pet owner is a big responsibility. I don't know if I'm cut out for it.'

'It's not your fault,' Rex assured him. 'The rest of the Mirror Pack are acting kinda nuts, too. The doc's got Seal knocked out and strapped to a table up in the lab, and Six is trying to beat some sense into Dan Nice downstairs somewhere.' He gave his friend an encouraging smile. 'Compared to the job we've been doing, I'd say you've looked after these guys pretty well.'

'Thanks,' Noah replied. 'But we can't keep them locked up forever, can we?'

Rex shook his head. 'No.'

'So, what do we do?'

'I don't know,' Rex admitted. He started to walk towards the elevator. 'But I know someone who does.'

Van Kleiss and Biowulf stood watching on as Breach smashed mirror after mirror in her wild rage.

'Want me to stop her?' Biowulf asked. He was

still hurting from the uppercut he'd received earlier, and was looking forward to taking his revenge on the four-armed girl.

'Not yet,' said Van Kleiss. They had searched hundreds of the mirrors for a way out, and now it was becoming difficult to keep track of which ones they had searched. 'Skalamander,' he said. 'Give Breach a helping hand. Destroy the mirrors. *All* of them.'

Dr Holiday slid another needle into Seal's arm and pushed down the plunger. A blue liquid swirled into the sleeping girl's veins.

'I hope you know what you're doing,' Holiday said.

'Doc, I *always* know what I'm doing,' Rex told her. She fixed him with a withering stare. 'OK, I *occasionally* know what I'm doing.'

'Well, I hope this is one of those occasions, Rex,' Holiday said. 'She's waking up.'

Rex and Noah looked down in time to see Seal's eyelids flutter open. They had covered every reflective surface before Holiday had given the injection, in the hope that it would stop her freaking out again.

'Wh-where am I?' Seal asked.

'You're having a lie-down,' Holiday said, softly.

'You kinda lost your mind for a while there,' Rex said, not quite so delicately. 'Smashed a mirror, smashed a metal door, tried to beat me to death. Ring any bells?'

Seal shook her head. 'OMG,' she said, hoarsely. 'I don't remember any of it.'

'Something's happening to you, and to the others, too,' Rex told her. 'It's like you're losing control and becoming ... evil. I have to figure out how to stop it.'

'You can't,' Seal said. 'Not here.'

'Not here? Where, then?'

Seal looked away. 'I can feel it, you know? Inside me. This ... this anger. It's like there's a darkness in my head that's trying to take control. When I saw my reflection, it became too strong. It took over.'

'How can we stop it?' Rex asked. 'How can we make you better?'

'You can't stop it. You can't make us better,' Seal told him. Her voice was hoarse, like she'd start crying at any moment. 'You can only send us back.'

'How can we send you back?' Rex asked.

'The Hall of Mirrors,' Seal whispered. 'You have to take us to the Hall of Mirrors.'

Rex wasn't so sure about that. 'I don't know,' he frowned. 'Both you and Dan Nice freaked out majorly the last time you saw mirrors. Going to a *hall* of them sounds like a bad idea.'

'It's the only way,' the girl whimpered. 'Dan Nice lied. Our world is nothing like this one. It's dark and it's scary, but at least there we're ourselves.

'This world is twisting us, turning us into something we're not,' she explained. Her fingers opened and Rex placed his hand in hers. 'You have to take us back to the Hall of Mirrors, Rex. You have to send us home!'

CHAPTER 16

THE PROVIDENCE TANK trundled through the fairground, sending people running for cover in all directions. Armed Agents jogged alongside the vehicle, barking orders for everyone to keep back.

Evening was drawing in over the fun fair, and the sky was a dark, ominous shade of grey. The light of a full moon tried to force its way through the clouds, but failed miserably.

Inside the tank, Rex and Noah sat with the Mirror Pack. Seal and Dan Nice were sitting silently, not quite their old selves, but not trying to kill anyone, either. Biowoof was scraping at the clear walls of his box, but his barking and snarling had stopped for the moment. Mandy was still invisible, so what she was doing was a mystery to all of them.

The tank rumbled to a halt and the driver shouted back from up front. 'We're here.'

'OK,' said Rex, unclipping his safety harness. 'I guess this is it.'

He and Noah stood up. Noah carried both boxes while Rex led Seal and Dan Nice out through the tank's side door. An icy wind blew past them as they stepped up to the entrance of the Hall of Mirrors.

'This seemed more fun last time,' Noah muttered.

Rex nodded in agreement. 'Yeah, it's kinda lost that party atmosphere, hasn't it?'

'Let's get this over with,' Dan Nice said, abruptly. He stepped through the doors and into the mirror house. Seal hesitated, wringing her hands together nervously. Eventually, though, she summoned all her courage and went inside.

'Uh, do you mind if I stay out here?' Noah asked. 'It's been a stressful day and I don't know if my nerves can handle any more weirdness right now.'

Rex smirked. 'Chicken,' he said.

'*Buck, buck, buck,*' Noah replied. 'If you get into trouble, shout me.'

'What'll you do, lay an egg?' Rex teased.

Noah laughed nervously, then held up the handles of the plastic boxes. Rex took them, gave his friend a brief nod, then stepped into the Hall of Mirrors behind Dan Nice and Seal.

The room Rex entered was dimly lit, and he could only just make out the closest mirror. The person looking back at him was short and stocky, with a head that looked completely flat on top. Was it a reflection, or was that person really in there somewhere, trapped forever behind the glass?

With a shudder, Rex stepped further into the room. The mirrors had been moved around since they'd last been here. Row after row of them were laid out in circles, every one pointing towards the centre of the hall.

The boxes Rex carried both began to shake as Biowoof and the now-visible Mandy hurled themselves against the ceilings and walls. 'Calm down, guys,' Rex said. 'It's just your reflection.' But the animals kept thrashing around, and Rex was forced to sit the boxes on the floor in case he dropped them.

It took him a few moments to find Seal and Dan Nice. They were standing between two rows of mirrors, holding onto one another, their eyes screwed tightly shut.

'Are you sure about this?' Rex asked. 'Isn't there some other way we can help you?'

'No, there is no other way,' Dan said. 'Even now, I can feel the darkness corrupting me, chewing through my insides. I can sense your nanites, and it is taking all of my will to resist trying to absorb them all.'

'He's right,' Seal said. 'Your world is beautiful, but it isn't ours. We need to go back to our world, or there's no saying what we'll do.'

Rex nodded. 'OK,' he said. 'What do you need me to do?'

'Help us find the mirror we came through,' Seal said. 'I ... I think I can open the portal again.'

'Um, that might be tricky,' Rex said, looking around at the mirrors. 'It looks like someone's been busy reorganising.'

'Then we must look for ourselves,' Dan said, grimly. 'It is the only way.'

'Won't that make you, you know, go crazy?' Rex asked.

'There is a very good chance that it will,' Dan told him, 'so we must move quickly. Lead us to the centre of the room.'

Rex took hold of their arms and guided them right into the middle of the circle. Fifty or sixty distorted versions of them appeared inside every mirror. Rex took a step back.

'OK,' he said. 'You can look now.'

Dan hissed and Seal sobbed as they flicked open their eyes. They spun on the spot, back to back, wilting beneath the accusing stares of their own twisted reflections.

'N-no,' Dan yelped. 'Too much. T-too much. Can't contain it.'

'Hold it together,' Rex urged. 'You can do it. Find the mirror.'

'C-can't,' Seal whispered. The muscles on her forearms began to bulge like blisters on her skin. 'Must ... smash ...'

'No smashing,' Rex said. 'You're meant to be looking now. Look for the mirror you came through. You said you could find it.'

A shriek of rage burst from Seal's lips. She made a move towards Rex, her hands balled into fists. Before she took more than a single step, though, she stopped. A sweat broke out across her forehead as she raised an arm and pointed to one of the mirrors at the edge of the first circle.

'Th-there,' she said through gritted teeth.
'The portal's in there!'

CHAPTER 17

'**D**O IT, SEAL,' Rex said. Beside the girl, Dan Nice was thrashing around, gripped by an overwhelming rage. From somewhere in the shadows, Rex heard the snapping of plastic, as Biowoof and Mandy tore free of their boxes. 'Do it now!'

Seal raised two shaky arms and tried to push back the fury flooding through her veins. A small red dot appeared in the centre of the mirror. In a second it had doubled in size. It kept doubling with every second that passed, until it filled the whole mirror from top to bottom.

'You did it,' Rex cheered, before being interrupted by a loud growl from behind him.

Spinning around, Rex found himself staring at a large brown dog. Patches of purple metal shone through its short fur, and long black claws sprouted from each of its four paws. Biowoof opened his mouth, revealing two rows of razor-sharp fangs.

Rex gulped. 'Grandma, what big teeth you have.'

Something large and scaly and semi-transparent crawled across the floor beside the dog. Mandy had grown to the size of a crocodile. Her jaws opened and snapped shut, sending a ripple of visibility along her entire body.

'And as for that?' Rex said. 'That's just plain terrifying.'

Rex didn't dare take his eyes off the mutated animals. He turned his head slightly and whispered to Seal, 'You know you guys are free to leave any time you like, right? Any time you want to take these things away, just go right ahead.'

'Oh, I don't think so,' Dan Nice growled back at him.

The foam finger struck Rex on the side of the head. It was one of the hardest blows he'd ever felt. He stumbled forwards, directly towards the gaping jaws of Biowoof.

Rex's Boogie Pack extended from his shoulders. The turbines fired, giving him just enough lift to leap over the heads of the two animals. But the room was too tight to fly around, and Rex had no choice but to cut the power and drop back to the ground.

He turned to find all four of the Mirror Pack looking back at him. Dan Nice stood at the front, with Biowoof crouched down low by his side. Seal's blonde hair hung down over her face, and her arms looked more muscular than ever.

Mandy was completely visible now, but Rex really wished she wasn't. She looked like a fight between a crocodile and a dinosaur, with teeth and scales and claws jutting out in every direction.

'Four against one?' Rex muttered. 'Shouldn't be too difficult.'

A movement through the mirror portal made Rex think again. He groaned loudly, knowing all too well what was coming next.

'Well, well, well,' said Van Kleiss, as he and the real Pack slid out from within the mirror. 'Isn't this cosy?'

'Hey, I have an idea,' Rex said, cheerfully. 'How about you guys just fight it out amongst yourselves and leave me out of this?'

As one, both Packs lunged for him. Rex leapt backwards, barely avoiding the outstretched hands of Van Kleiss and his mirror counterpart.

'No?' Rex said. 'Well, trust me ...' he began.

With a *clank*, the Big Freakin' Sword appeared in his hand. '... you're not going to like the alternative, either.'

REX SWUNG WITH THE SWORD, only to find it blocked by Skalamander's diamond-hard club hand. Mandy's tail whipped out, knocking Rex's feet away. He retracted the sword and rolled clumsily on the ground, just as hot, sticky saliva began to pour down around him.

Rex twisted, firing a kick against the side of Biowoof's head. 'Down, boy,' he said, but the dog barely flinched. Rex gritted his teeth. He knew what he had to do. There was nothing else for it.

'Heeeeeeelp!' he cried. 'Noooooah!'

Van Kleiss dragged Rex to his feet. He and Dan Nice spoke at exactly the same time.

'You think your little friend can help you now?' they said, in perfect unison.

'Jinx, can't speak until I say your name,' Rex told them.

'What are you talking about?' they both muttered. Rex punched them both hard on the arm. 'You broke the jinx,' he said. 'You have to take the punishment. I don't make the rules.'

All eight of Rex's opponents made a move towards him. 'Wait, wait!' he cried. 'You asked me if I thought Noah could help me. Well, no, I don't.' He pointed behind the Packs. 'But I bet those guys can.'

The villains turned to find eight Providence Agents standing in the doorway, all dressed in identical uniforms. As the Agents marched in, their reflections filled the mirrors, making the room appear full of them.

'Looks like the cavalry has arrived,' Rex smiled, before he brought out the Smackhands and knocked all eight Pack members backwards towards the centre of the room.

'Split up,' Van Kleiss spat. 'Take out the Agents, I'll deal with Rex.'

Skalamander raised his club arm and sprayed deadly diamond shards towards an Agent's back. There was a tinkling of breaking glass and the Agent shattered into pieces.

'That was a mirror, you idiot,' Biowulf snarled. 'Attack the *real* Agents. Like *this*!'

He hurled himself at another of the Agents, his claws fully outstretched. His arm came down sharply, cutting through the Agent's chest.

CRACK.

'Another mirror?' Biowulf spluttered, barely able to believe he'd made the same mistake as Skalamander.

One of the real Agents opened fire with his machine-gun. The bullets narrowly missed Biowulf and turned three more mirrors into shards of glass.

Rex saw Biowoof stagger sideways, suddenly disorientated. More gunshots rang out, another mirror exploded, and the mutant dog let out a yelp of shock.

'The mirrors,' Rex realised. 'Take out the mirrors!'

'What? No!' Dan snarled. He threw himself at Rex, attacking him with the rock-hard foam finger. 'That's not *nice*, and I should know,' he hissed, right up close in Rex's face. 'Because Dan Nice knows nice!'

'And Rex knows kicking butt,' Rex replied. He shoved Dan backwards. The mirror-man stumbled across the room, before crashing into a mirror. It toppled slowly and knocked into the next mirror. They fell like dominoes, taking half a dozen more mirrors with them.

'No!' Dan wailed. 'No, no, n–'

And then, with a faint *pop*, Dan disappeared.

The sound of machine-gun fire ripped around the room, forcing Rex to cover his ears. Glass sprayed in every direction, like a deadly downpour of rain.

POP!

Mandy disappeared next, not gradually, like when she turned invisible, but suddenly, and all at once.

POP!

Biowoof gave a puzzled *yap* before he vanished completely.

Van Kleiss could see which way that battle was turning. 'Breach!' he yelled. 'Get us out of here!'

Before Rex could stop her, Breach summoned another portal. There was only one mirror left intact in the room, and it didn't interfere with the portal this time.

'Until we meet again,' Van Kleiss growled, as he and his Pack leapt through the swirling red hole and back to Abysus.

Rex turned and looked at the last remaining member of the Mirror Pack. She was standing before the last remaining mirror, inside which Rex could see the swirling portal she had created earlier.

'Seven down,' Rex sighed. 'One to go.'

CHAPTER 19

REX STOOD FACING SEAL, a few metres away. The girl's arms were still bulging, and her hair was still hanging down over her face, but she wasn't showing any sign that she was about to attack.

'I'm sorry this happened to you,' Rex told her.

'N-not your fault,' Seal hissed. Even the effort of speaking seemed to be taking its toll on her.

'The others. What happened to them when the mirrors broke?' asked Rex.

'Back to Mirror World,' Seal said, hoarsely. 'Trapped down there in the cold and in the dark.'

'I'm sorry,' Rex said again.

'Not your fault, either.' There was a long pause before Seal spoke again. 'There is a R-Rex in my world, too,' she said.

Rex felt his eyebrows raise in surprise. 'There is? What's he like?'

Seal shrugged her skinny shoulders. 'Not nearly as much fun as you are.'

'That's good to know,' Rex smiled.

It was Seal's turn to apologise. 'S-sorry for the trouble we caused,' she said. 'We never m-meant to hurt anyone.'

'Forget it,' Rex said. 'Like, *totally*.'

A brief flicker of a smile passed across Seal's face. 'I'm ready to go home now,' she wheezed. She held up a hand. 'Goodbye, Rex.'

'Goodbye, Seal,' Rex said. He watched as she turned and walked towards the mirror. For a moment it looked like she was going to bump into the glass surface, but then she was stepping through it and vanishing into the portal.

Rex waited for a few seconds, in case she came back. She didn't. He turned to the three Agents standing on his left. 'Shoot it,' he said, his throat tight. 'Destroy the mirror so they don't come back.'

'Yes, sir,' barked one of the Agents. All three of them raised their weapons.

Deep in the portal, Rex saw something move. He peered into its swirling dark heart and there, looking back at him, was someone who looked almost exactly like himself. There were three figures standing around him, but they weren't Agents. They were a man and a woman, and a boy a little older than he was. The way they stood around the mirror Rex made them look almost like ... family?

'Wait!' Rex cried, but he gave the order too late. Three fingers twitched on three triggers and a hail of bullets turned the glass in the mirror to fragments. Rex dropped to his knees and picked at the shards, staring into them, hoping to see his mirror-self looking back.

But all he saw was his own warped reflection. He let the glass pieces fall to the floor. Silently, he turned and left the Hall of Mirrors behind.

'Hey, you OK?' Noah asked, as Rex passed him.

Rex paused at the door to the tank. He looked back at the mirror house and finally shook his head. 'I don't know,' he admitted. 'I really don't know.'

The two friends climbed back into the tank, neither one saying any more. The door closed over with a loud *clang*, the engines growled, and they began the long, bumpy ride back to Providence Base.

CHAPTER 20

WHEN REX SHUFFLED OUT of the elevator, Dr Holiday put her arms around him and pulled him into a hug.

'What was that for?' he asked, when she'd let go.

'You looked like you need it,' she replied. 'Rough night, huh?'

'Yeah,' Rex admitted. 'You could say that. The Mirror Pack's back where they belong.'

Holiday smiled, encouragingly. 'You did well, Rex.'

'Did I?' he frowned. 'Then why do I feel so bad about it?'

'Because you're a nice guy,' she told him.

Rex shuddered. '*Nice*? Please, can we not use that word from now on?'

Holiday nodded. 'Deal,' she said. 'Now, Bobo's in his room. He ordered Chinese food for you guys. My treat.'

'Thanks, Doc,' Rex said. 'But I think I'm just going to bed. Like you say, it's been a rough night, and

I could do with putting it all behind me.'

Dr Holiday looked concerned. 'Are you sure?' she asked. 'Maybe company's the best thing for you. It's probably not a good idea to be alone right now.'

'It's OK,' Rex told her. 'I won't be alone.'

Rex sat on the end of his bed, staring straight ahead. Another Rex looked back, identical in every way. Rex raised his arm. The other Rex raised his at exactly the same time.

A reflection. Just a reflection.

'Hello?' he said, feeling stupid. 'I, uh, I don't know if you can hear me in there. I saw you earlier, but then the mirror broke and ...' His voice trailed off.

'I wish I knew who those people I saw you with were. They looked like they cared about you. That must be n–' He stopped himself before he said the word. '*Awesome*. That must be awesome.' Rex chuckled, sadly. 'Like, OMG, *totally*.'

'Talking to yourself again?'

Rex stared into the mirror, before realising that the voice had come from over by the door. Agent

Six stood there in his immaculate green suit, his eyes hidden beneath mirrored sunglasses.

'Uh, yeah, I guess I must've been,' Rex said.

'Just wanted to tell you I think you did a good job out there,' Six said. 'It couldn't have been easy. You handled it well.'

'Hey, that's two compliments in one night, Six. Are you sure you're not a mirror alter-ego?'

'Pretty sure,' Six said. 'But if I am, I know I can count on you to do the right thing.'

Rex nodded gratefully. 'Thanks, Six,' he said.

'Don't mention it.' The Agent walked on, leaving Rex alone with the mirror. A moment later, Six's head appeared around the doorframe again. 'And, Rex?' he said. 'Don't sit staring at your own reflection all night. People will start to think you're vain.'

'I was just ... looking for something,' Rex told him.

'Well, whatever it is, I'm sure you'll find it eventually,' Six replied.

Rex looked into the mirror. 'Yeah,' he said, at long last. 'I really hope I will.'

'Goodnight, Rex.'

Rex stood up. 'Goodnight, Six,' he said. Then,

with a final longing look at his reflection, Rex pulled back his covers, slipped into bed, and drifted off into a deep, dreamless sleep.

TOTAL RECALL

Test your memory of 'Mirror Mirror' with these eight tricky questions. Remember: no checking back!

1 The Wheel of Terror is what kind of fairground ride?
a. Spinning teacups
b. Merry-go-round
c. Big Wheel

2 What is the golden prize on the test-your-strength machine?
a. A bar of gold
b. A goldfish
c. A gold watch

3 Which member of The Pack is pulled first into the mirror portal?
a. Biowulf
b. Breach
c. Van Kleiss

4 What breed of dog is Biowoof?
a. Great Dane
b. Alsatian
c. Labrador

5 Who does Six send to Chicago on a mission with Rex?
a. Dan Nice
b. Seal
c. Dr Holiday

6 What is the name of the reflective sculpture that Rex sees in Chicago?
a. The Moon Gate
b. The Cloud Gate
c. The Star Gate

7 How many Agents are sent into the Hall of Mirrors to help Rex?
a. Four
b. Eight
c. Sixteen

8 Who is the last member of the Mirror Pack to go back through the portal?
a. Dan Nice
b. Biowoof
c. Seal

Read an exclusive sneak preview of

GENERATOR REX: THE TRADE

FLUUUB!

HIGH ON A GRASSY VERGE in San Francisco's Golden Gate Park, something was growing. It was a man. At least, it *had* been.

His arms and legs were swelling, puffing up until they were several times their normal width. His whole body bulged, growing larger and more bloated with every second that passed.

Other park visitors began to scream and wail and run for their lives, as the man's skin became slick and gloopy and his limbs were drawn into his now bus-sized body.

Inside him, microscopic machines called nanites were altering his molecular structure, turning him from a human being into something new.

And into something *revolting*.

Rex yawned. He was curled up on a chair inside a Providence tank, wishing he were still in bed.

'Eight a.m.?' he groaned. 'Seriously? Who goes to the park at eight a.m.?'

Over by the door, Agent Six jabbed a series of buttons. 'Half of San Francisco,' he snapped, 'so we need to keep civilian casualties to a minimum.' He turned and glared at Rex through his sunglasses. 'Which means I need you awake.'

'I'm awake!' Rex protested. He stood up, stretched, then yawned again. 'But seriously — *eight a.m.*? Someone needs to teach these Evos how to tell time.'

Agent Six flicked a final switch and the door slid open. The sound of screaming and gunfire immediately filled the inside of the tank. Six stepped aside. 'Be my guest,' he said, motioning for Rex to lead the way.

'Ew,' Rex winced as he stepped down from the tank, 'what stinks?' He looked up and spotted the giant slug-like monster squirming on the grass just twenty or so metres away. 'Oh. Yeah. Forget I asked.'

Gunfire roared around them as a squadron of Providence Agents opened fire on the Evo. The Agents' bullets passed through the creature's jelly-like body, before emerging harmlessly on the other side.

A woman in a white lab coat stormed out from within the tank. 'Tell them to stop shooting,' Dr Holiday barked. 'That thing's unstable. Hit it in the wrong place and it pops like a balloon, then everyone here gets covered in nanite soup.'

Six raised an arm. The sound of gunfire immediately stopped.

Dr Holiday sighed with relief. '*Thank* you.'

'Looks like it's all down to you, kid,' said Six.

'So, what's new?' Rex asked. 'Anything special I need to know?'

'Don't get killed.'

'Thanks,' replied Rex. 'I'll bear that in mind.'

With a *whirr* and a *clank*, he put the nanites within his own body into action. Two enormous robotic fists grew from Rex's arms. He clanked them together a couple of times, testing them, then ran closer to the wriggling slug-beast.

'Hey, Gloopy,' Rex cried. He pointed to a small "KEEP OFF THE GRASS" sign sticking out of the ground. 'Can't you read?'

BEEEUUUK!

The Evo's mouth opened and a spray of bright

green gunk erupted from inside it. The gunk hit the sign, turning it into a sizzling pile of goo.

'OK,' Rex said, 'I'm going to take that as a "no".'

Raising a metal fist, Rex charged. One good, solid punch should be enough to knock the Evo out, he reckoned. After that, the rest would be easy.

Halfway there, Dr Holiday's voice crackled in his ear. 'Pop like a balloon, *remember*?'

'What? You mean I can't even – Whoa!'

Another spray of green slime spewed at him. His robotic arms retracted back into his body and a pair of jet turbines extended from his shoulders. With a *roar*, the Boogie Pack lifted into the air just as the grass at his feet dissolved in a puddle of sludge.

'So, we can't shoot it *or* hit it?' Rex asked, climbing higher above the park.

Dr Holiday's voice buzzed in his ear. 'No. We can't risk it spreading more nanites.'

Rex looked down. The slug Evo was squelching across the grass towards the Providence soldiers.

'I'd say reasoning with it is out of the question, too,' Rex muttered. He took a deep breath. 'Guess I'm just going to have to get my hands dirty.'

WHOOSH!

Rex rocketed towards the Evo, his face fixed in a mask of determination. This was going to get nasty!

As he passed above the slug-beast, he folded the jetpack back into his body. Almost at once he began to fall. Only the gloopy hide of the Evo stopped him hitting the ground.

Mechanical feet grew from Rex's legs, allowing him to grip onto the Evo's back, like a cowboy on a bucking bronco. The Evo growled as Rex pressed his hands against the monster's slimy skin.

'Trust me,' he grimaced, 'I don't like this any more than you do.'

Concentrating hard, Rex absorbed the nanites from inside the Evo. He felt them flow into his body, and as they did, the slug-creature became a slug-man, and then, finally, just a man.

Standing up, Rex wiped his sticky hands on the front of his trousers. 'Another one bites the ... um ... slime.'

Retracting his Punk Buster legs back into his body, Rex turned to find Agent Six standing in front of him. He was about to speak when the Punk Busters emerged again all on their own. 'Whoa, where'd they come from?' he frowned.

Agent Six raised an eyebrow. 'Everything OK?'

'Yeah, it's just –'

The legs pulled back into Rex's body. He paused for a moment, making sure they were gone for good this time. 'Weird,' he began, but a sudden *clanking* sound stopped him. The Punk Busters reformed yet again, only this time it was clear that something was very wrong.

Rex stared at his arms, which now had a huge pair of mechanical feet attached to the end of them. 'OK,' he swallowed. 'This is *not* good.'